GOOD SPORTS PLAY FAIR

By BREANN RUMSCH

Illustrated by MIKE PETRIK

Music by MARK OBLINGER

CANTATA
LEARNING

WWW.CANTATALEARNING.COM

CANTATA
LEARNING

Published by Cantata Learning
1710 Roe Crest Drive
North Mankato, MN 56003
www.cantatalearning.com

Library of Congress Cataloging-in-Publication Data

Names: Rumsch, BreAnn, 1981- author. | Petrik, Mike, illustrator. |
   Oblinger, Mark, composer.
Title: Good sports play fair / by BreAnn Rumsch ; illustrated by Mike Petrik
   ; music by Mark Oblinger.
Description: North Mankato, MN : Cantata Learning, [2019] | "This text is
   set to the tune of 'This Old Man'." | Includes bibliographical references. |
   Audience: Ages: 5-7. | Audience: Grades: K-3.
Identifiers: LCCN 2018053374 (print) | LCCN 2019000079 (ebook) | ISBN
   9781684104161 (eBook) | ISBN 9781684104017 (hardcover) | ISBN
   9781684104284 (pbk.)
Subjects: LCSH: Sportsmanship--Juvenile literature. | Flag football--Juvenile literature.
Classification: LCC GV706.3 (ebook) | LCC GV706.3 .R85 2019 (print) | DDC
   175--dc23
LC record available at https://lccn.loc.gov/2018053374

Book design and art direction: Tim Palin Creative
Editorial direction: Kellie M. Hultgren
Music direction: Elizabeth Draper
Music arranged and produced by Mark Oblinger

Printed in the United States of America.
0406

This text is set to the tune of "This Old Man."

ACCESS THE MUSIC!

SCAN
CODE
WITH
MOBILE
APP

CANTATALEARNING.COM

TIPS TO SUPPORT LITERACY AT HOME

WHY READING AND SINGING WITH YOUR CHILD IS SO IMPORTANT

Daily reading with your child leads to increased academic achievement. Music and songs, specifically rhyming songs, are a fun and easy way to build early literacy and language development. Music skills correlate significantly with both phonological awareness and reading development. Singing helps build vocabulary and speech development. And reading and appreciating music together is a wonderful way to strengthen your relationship.

READ AND SING EVERY DAY!

TIPS FOR USING CANTATA LEARNING BOOKS AND SONGS DURING YOUR DAILY STORY TIME

1. As you sing and read, point out the different words on the page that rhyme. Suggest other words that rhyme.

2. Memorize simple rhymes such as Itsy Bitsy Spider and sing them together. This encourages comprehension skills and early literacy skills.

3. Use the questions in the back of each book to guide your singing and storytelling.

4. Read the included sheet music with your child while you listen to the song. How do the music notes correlate to the words of the song?

5. Sing along on the go and at home. Access music by scanning the QR code on each Cantata book. You can also stream or download the music for free to your computer, smartphone, or mobile device.

Devoting time to daily reading shows that you are available for your child. Together, you are building language, literacy, and listening skills.

Have fun reading and singing!

What does it mean to play **fair**? It means that you know and follow the rules of the game. It means that you show **respect** to your **coach** and to other players. Sometimes it might seem like it would be better to **cheat**. But cheating can hurt you or others.

When you **choose** to play fair, you are being a good sport. When everyone plays fair, everyone can have more fun. To see what happens when some football players learn about playing fair, turn the page and sing along!

Time to play! We will share.
We won't cheat. We're playing fair.

When you cheat,
the game is no fun for anyone.
Playing fair is much more fun.

Grownups teach us what to do.
We start out by learning rules.

When you cheat,
the game is no fun for anyone.
Playing fair is much more fun.

Rules help keep us safe, you see.

No one wants an **injury**.

When you cheat,

the game is no fun for anyone.

Playing fair is much more fun.

There's a **foul**! The whistle blows.
If someone cheats, the whole field knows.

When you cheat,
the game is no fun for anyone.
Playing fair is much more fun.

Breaking rules is not allowed.

Playing right makes our coach **proud**.

When you cheat,

the game is no fun for anyone.

Playing fair is much more fun.

If we mess up, we don't fight.
We step up to make it right.

When you cheat,
the game is no fun for anyone.
Playing fair is much more fun.

Take the field with the rest.
Try again and play your best.

When you cheat,
the game is no fun for anyone.
Playing fair is much more fun.

Win or lose, we don't care.

We feel proud when we play fair.

When you cheat,

the game is no fun for anyone.

Playing fair is much more fun.

Fair means fun for everyone!

SONG LYRICS
Good Sports Play Fair

Time to play! We will share.
We won't cheat. We're playing fair.
When you cheat,
the game is no fun for anyone.
Playing fair is much more fun.

Grownups teach us what to do.
We start out by learning rules.
When you cheat,
the game is no fun for anyone.
Playing fair is much more fun.

Rules help keep us safe, you see.
No one wants an injury.
When you cheat,
the game is no fun for anyone.
Playing fair is much more fun.

There's a foul! The whistle blows.
If someone cheats, the whole field knows.
When you cheat,
the game is no fun for anyone.
Playing fair is much more fun.

Breaking rules is not allowed.
Playing right makes our coach proud.
When you cheat,
the game is no fun for anyone.
Playing fair is much more fun.

If we mess up, we don't fight.
We step up to make it right.
When you cheat,
the game is no fun for anyone.
Playing fair is much more fun.

Take the field with the rest.
Try again and play your best.
When you cheat,
the game is no fun for anyone.
Playing fair is much more fun.

Win or lose, we don't care.
We feel proud when we play fair.
When you cheat,
the game is no fun for anyone.
Playing fair is much more fun.

Fair means fun for everyone!

Good Sports Play Fair

World
Mark Oblinger

1. Time to play! We will share. We won't cheat. We're play-ing fair. When you cheat, the game is no fun for an-y-one.

Play-ing fair is much more fun.

Fair means fun for eve-ry - one!

Verse 2
Grownups teach us what to do.
We start out by learning rules.
When you cheat,
the game is no fun for anyone.
Playing fair is much more fun.

Verse 3
Rules help keep us safe, you see.
No one wants an injury.
When you cheat,
the game is no fun for anyone.
Playing fair is much more fun.

Verse 4
There's a foul! The whistle blows.
If someone cheats, the whole field knows.
When you cheat,
the game is no fun for anyone.
Playing fair is much more fun.

Verse 5
Breaking rules is not allowed.
Playing right makes our coach proud.
When you cheat,
the game is no fun for anyone.
Playing fair is much more fun.

Verse 6
If we mess up, we don't fight.
We step up to make it right.
When you cheat,
the game is no fun for anyone.
Playing fair is much more fun.

Verse 7
Take the field with the rest.
Try again and play your best.
When you cheat,
the game is no fun for anyone.
Playing fair is much more fun.

Verse 8
Win or lose, we don't care.
We feel proud when we play fair.
When you cheat,
the game is no fun for anyone.
Playing fair is much more fun.

(spoken) Fair means fun for everyone!

GLOSSARY

cheat—to break a rule

choose—to pick one or the other

coach—a person who teaches sports

fair—the right way, where everyone gets the same chance

foul—a broken rule in a game

injury—what someone has if they get hurt

proud—very happy about something you have done

respect—a feeling that someone or something is important and should be valued

CRITICAL THINKING QUESTIONS

1. In the story, one of the football players breaks a game rule. Do you think he cheated? Why is cheating wrong? What kind of things can happen because of cheating?

2. Imagine that you cheated in a game and someone got hurt. Write a letter to the person who got hurt because you cheated. What do you need to tell them to make it right?

3. The kids in this book wear mouth guards when they play. How do you think mouth guards help them stay safe?

TO LEARN MORE

Arrow, Emily. *Making It Happen*. North Mankato, MN: Cantata Learning, 2020.

Doeden, Matt. *All About Football*. North Mankato, MN: A+ Books, 2015.

Dungy, Tony. *Austin Plays Fair: A Team Dungy Story About Football*. Eugene, OR: Harvest House, 2018.

Higgins, Melissa. *I Am Fair*. North Mankato, MN: Pebble Books, 2014.

Moore, Elizabeth. *Sports Rules*. North Mankato, MN: Wonder Readers, 2014.